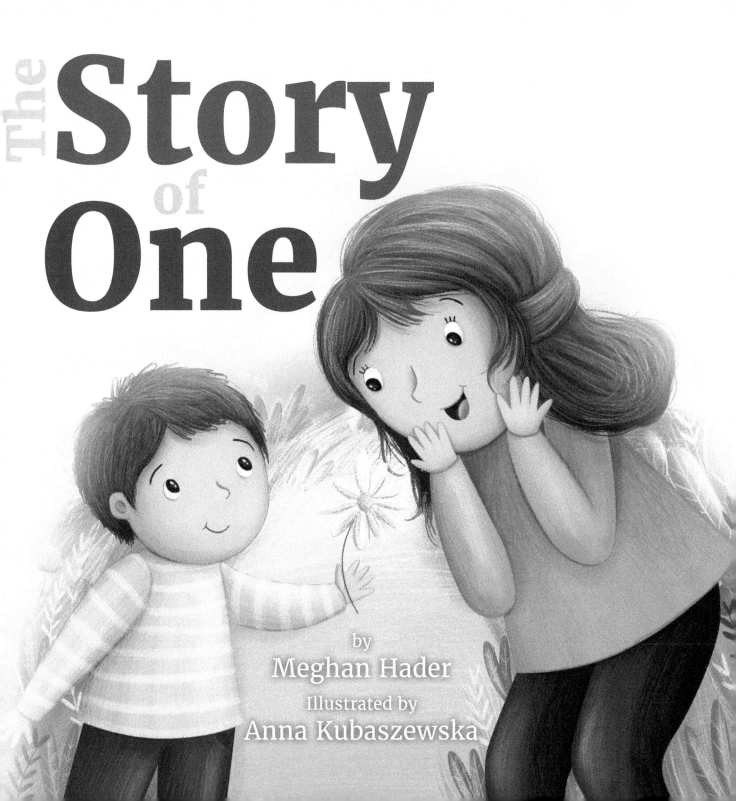

The Story of One

of

by
Meghan Hader

Illustrated by
Anna Kubaszewska

ISBN: 978-1-954614-48-2 (hard cover)
      978-1-954614-49-9 (soft cover)
Editing: Amy Ashby

Warren
publishing

Published by Warren Publishing
Charlotte, NC
www.warrenpublishing.net
Printed in the United States

For my family, friends,
and students past and present;
and to all who choose to do just one

With one little penny, a small, simple coin,
a change can be made for a young girl or boy.

With one pretty flower, picked or bought,
you show a loved one they are in your thoughts.

With one quick swoop, one reach of the hand,
a beautiful park has one less can.

With one lovely card, a meaningful note,
someone's feelings are back afloat.

With one cool car, a neat little toy,
another child shares in the fun and joy.

But not every gift
must be something to touch.
Sometimes, giving *you*
is giving just as much.

So give one big grin, one amazing smile,
to show someone they are worth your while.

Send one powerful thought, a quick little prayer,
and have faith that your message is helping somewhere.

Terrace Avenue

Share your talents with others, your beautiful gifts,
and watch how spirits around you lift.

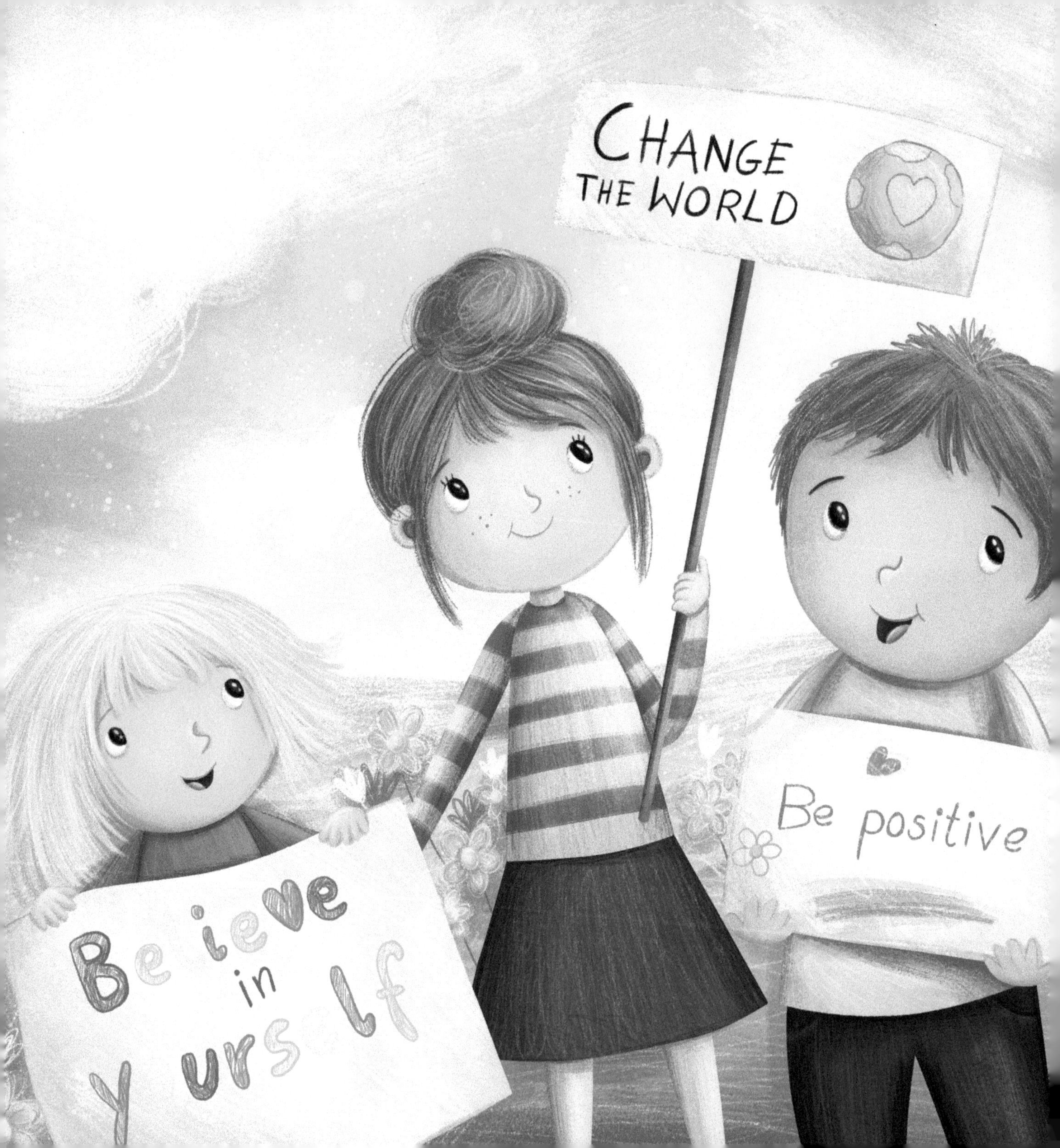
CHANGE THE WORLD
Be ieve in y urs lf
Be positive

Let the world hear your voice, so beautiful and true,
and stand up for what's right in all that you do.

You are BEAUTIFUL

Smile :)

NEVER give up

BELIEVE IN YOURSELF

YOU ARE NOT alone!

Give one kind word, one loving phrase,
and know you just made someone else's day.

The power of one
can go a long way,
so what's keeping you
from doing just *one* today?

CPSIA information can be obtained
at www.ICGtesting.com
Printed in the USA
LVHW071658081121
702779LV00007B/638